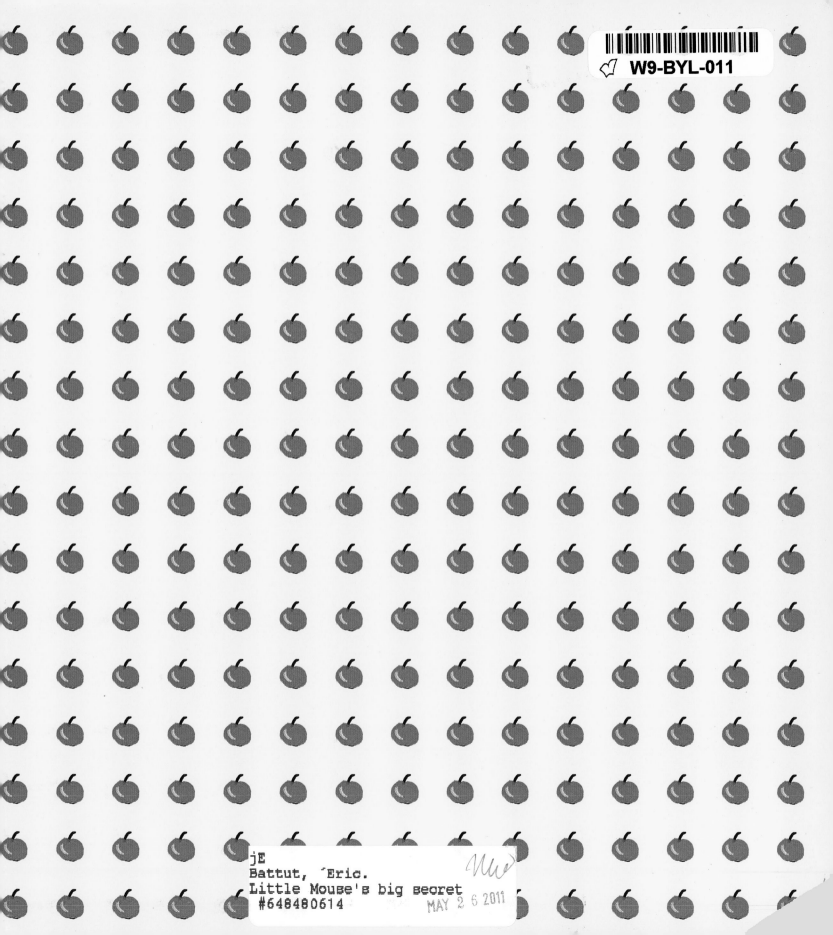

STERLING and the distinctive Sterling logo are
registered trademarks of Sterling Publishing Co., Inc.

Library of Congress Cataloging-in-Publication Data
Battut, Éric.
[Secret. English]
Little Mouse's big secret / by Éric Battut.
p. cm.
Summary: Little Mouse refuses to reveal his secret despite being questioned by his friends.
ISBN 978-1-4027-7462-1
[1. Secrets—Fiction. 2. Mice—Fiction. 3. Animals—Fiction.] I. Title.
PZ7.B32468Li 2011
[E] —dc22

2010019689

Lot#:
2 4 6 8 10 9 7 5 3
12/10
Published in 2011 by Sterling Publishing Co., Inc.
387 Park Avenue South, New York, NY 10016
Originally published in France under the title *Le Secret*
Copyright © 2004 by Didier Jeunesse, 8, rue d'Assas 75006 Paris
English translation © 2011 by Sterling Publishing Co., Inc.
The illustrations were created in oil paint.
Distributed in Canada by Sterling Publishing
c/o Canadian Manda Group, 165 Dufferin Street
Toronto, Ontario, Canada M6K 3H6
Distributed in the United Kingdom by GMC Distribution Services
Castle Place, 166 High Street, Lewes, East Sussex, England BN7 1XU
Distributed in Australia by Capricorn Link (Australia) Pty. Ltd.
P.O. Box 704, Windsor, NSW 2756, Australia

Sterling ISBN 978-1-4027-7462-1

For information about custom editions, special sales, premium and
corporate purchases, please contact Sterling Special Sales Department
at 800-805-5489 or specialsales@sterlingpublishing.com.

Designed by Katrina Damkoehler.

Little Mouse's
BIG
SECRET

by Éric Battut

STERLING
New York / London

Oh! What a delicious treat!

It will be my secret.

I will hide it.

"What are you hiding?" asked Squirrel.

"It's my secret, and I'll never tell," answered Mouse.

"What are you hiding?" asked Bird.

"It's my secret, and I'll never tell," answered Mouse.

"What are you hiding?" asked Turtle.

"It's my secret, and I'll never tell," answered Mouse.

"What are you hiding?" asked Hedgehog.

"It's my secret, and I'll never tell," answered Mouse.

"What are you hiding?" asked Rabbit.

"It's my secret, and I'll never tell," answered Mouse.

"What are you hiding?" asked Frog.

"It's my secret, and I'll never tell," answered Mouse.

I will keep my secret forever!

Uh-oh! My secret is out!

But sometimes . . . secrets are even better

when you share them.

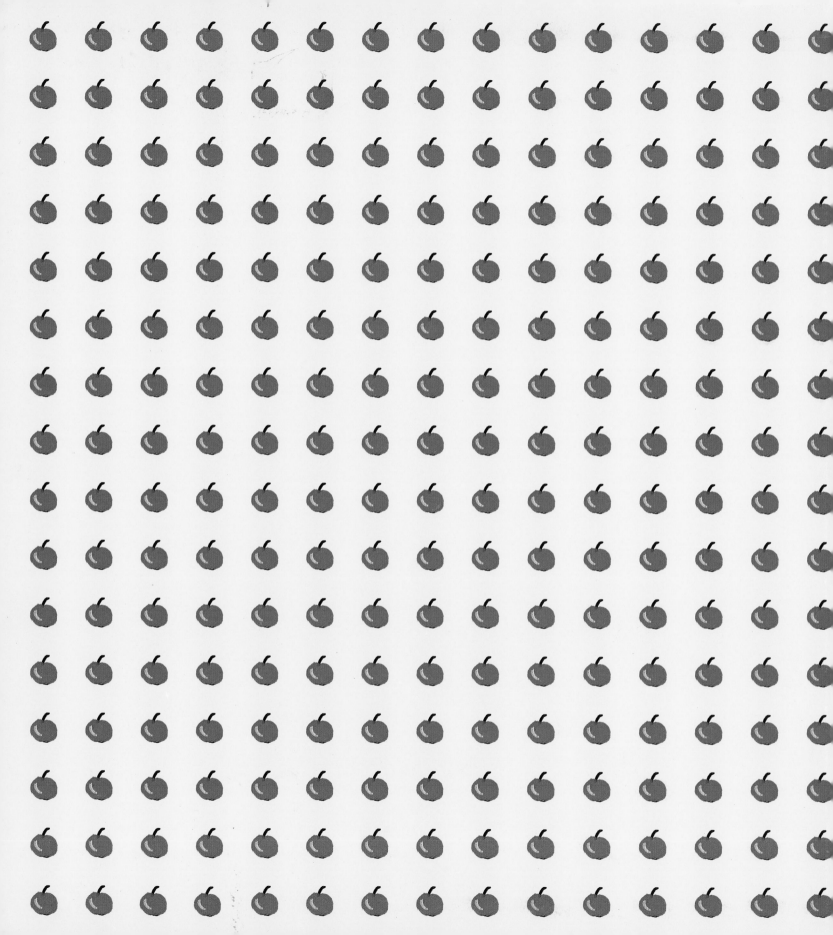